This Adventure
Belongs To:

....

For more information connect at www.jaimejangles.com
First edition Februrary, 2021

ISBN: 978-1-7774525-2-0
www.jaimejangles.com
@jaimejangles

This book is for all the
children and adults
with imaginations.

These are the stay-at-home adventures of Jaime Jangles and her Zany Dad Jeff.

Where would they start? They could go right or left.

The schools were all closed. It was stormy outside.

Sunnyside
Public School

Stay Dry, Stay Safe!

So they took their imaginations
for a rocketship ride.

They could go on a trip and fly through the air.

Or take a big boat if they have time to spare.

They could play all sorts of sports with broomsticks and balls.

They could dress up as painters and wear overalls.

They could press billions of buttons and learn how to type.

They could hand-pick fresh fruit from the trees when they're ripe.

They could look through old pictures
to remember the past.

They could sing out the alphabet
from first letter to last.

They could broadcast the news
and be journalists.

They could celebrate the big game
with the clench of their fists.

But when it was time for the day to be through,
they would fall into bed and sigh a big WHEW!

Today was so GREAT, but tomorrow WILL BE GRANDER!
Maybe cruise the Milky Way like a Starship Commander.

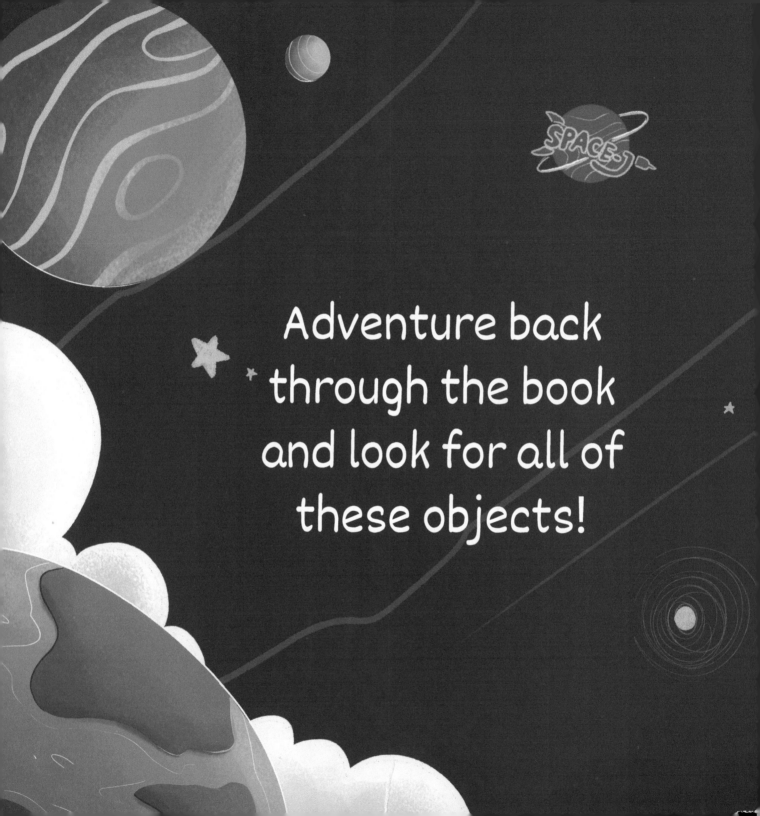

Adventure back
through the book
and look for all of
these objects!

Milk Box - 1

Red Car - 1

Duck - 2

Red Ball - 4

Umbrella - 1

Pizza Box - 1

Canadian Flag - 2

Pink Elephant - 24

Dustpan - 1

About the Author(s)

Day 1 of the Lurie "Lur"ning Academy in
Toronto, Canada started during some uncertain times in
2020. Jeff wrote a poem about a few stay-at-home
adventures he had experienced with his
4 year-old daughter Jaime.

Jaime didn't start kindergarten...
Instead, she immediately started her career
as her Dad's Creative Director!

They scoured online CVs from illustrators worldwide.
Jaime finally decided on Andy Yura
from East Java, Indonesia.

Together, they crafted the perfect blend of
real and imaginary worlds in a colourful and creative way.
They also had a blast placing Jaime's favourite snuggle toy
"Elefanté" on each page.

When they aren't working on "The Adventures of Jaime
Jangles", the father-daughter duo is hanging out with
Super-Mom Erin and new sister Casey Bea.

Jaime is a professional big sister
and Jeff is a Voice Director/Music Composer
and a Professional Doubles Squash Player.

Creative Director: Jaime Lurie
Written by: Jeff Lurie
Illustrated by: Andy Yura
Cover Design: Kyle Winsor
Final Layout & Inserts: Erin Lurie

Thanks to everyone that helped us with the Jangles creative process:
EL, CL, Mom, Dad, LR, DR, LR, DL, MS, KW, DW, CH, WS, CL, JM, JL, DS.

CPSIA information can be obtained
at www.ICGtesting.com
Printed in the USA
BVHW022252250421
605207BV00002B/11